Freckle Juice

Freckle Juice

JUDY BLUME

Illustrated by Sonia O. Lisker

A Yearling Book

Published by
Dell Publishing
a division of
Bantam Doubleday Dell Publishing Group, Inc.
666 Fifth Avenue
New York, New York 10103

ISBN: 0-440-42813-0

Reprinted by arrangement with Bradbury Press, an affiliate of Macmillan Inc.

Printed in the United States of America

One Previous edition

November 1986

70 69 68 67 66 65 64 63 62 61

CW

FOR RANDY . . .
My favorite freckle face

Freckle Juice

1

Andrew Marcus wanted freckles. Nicky Lane had freckles. He had about a million of them. They covered his face, his ears and the back of his neck. Andrew didn't have any freckles. He had two warts on his finger. But they didn't do him any good at all. If he had freckles like Nicky, his mother would never know if his neck was dirty. So he wouldn't have to wash. And then he'd never be late for school.

Andrew had plenty of time to look at Nicky's freckles. He sat right behind him in class. Once he even tried to count them. But when he got to eighty-six Miss Kelly called, "Andrew . . . are you paying attention?"

"Yes, Miss Kelly," Andrew said.

11

"Good, Andrew. I'm glad to hear that. Now will you please pick up your chair and join your reading group? We're all waiting for you."

Andrew stood up in a hurry. His reading group giggled. Especially Sharon. He couldn't stand that Sharon. She thought she knew everything! He picked up his chair and carried it to the corner where his reading group sat.

"You may begin, Andrew," Miss Kelly said. "Page sixty-four."

Andrew turned the pages in his book. Sixty-four . . . sixty-four. He couldn't find it. The pages stuck together. Why did Miss Kelly have to pick him?

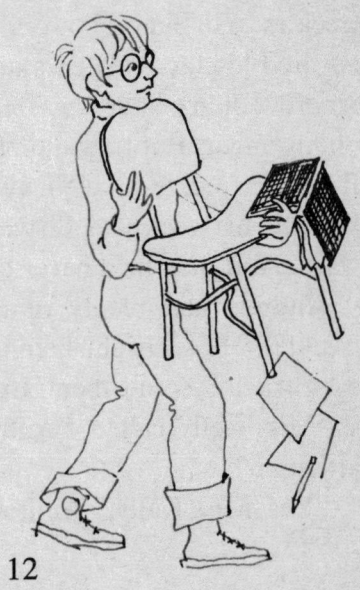

Everybody else already had their books opened to the right page.

Sharon kept giggling. She covered her mouth to keep in the noise, but Andrew knew what was going on. He finally found page sixty-four. Right where it was supposed to be . . . between pages sixty-three and sixty-five. If he had his own freckles he wouldn't have to count Nicky Lane's. Then he'd hear Miss Kelly when she called reading groups. And nobody would laugh at him.

Later, when the bell rang, Andrew poked Nicky Lane.

"What do you want?" Nicky asked, turning around.

"I was wondering about your freckles," Andrew said.

"Oh yeah? What about them?"

Andrew felt pretty stupid. "Well, how did you get them?"

"What do you mean *how?* You get *born* with them. That's how!"

Andrew thought that's what Nicky would say. Some help *he* was!

"Line up, boys and girls," Miss Kelly said. "Time to go home now. Sharon, you may lead the girls. Andrew, you may lead the boys."

Some luck! Just when he got to be leader he had to stand next to *Sharon!*

When they were in line Sharon whispered to Andrew. "Psst . . . I know how to get them."

"How to get what?" Andrew asked.

"Freckles," Sharon said.

"Who asked *you?*"

"I heard you ask Nicky about his." Sharon ran her tongue along her teeth. She was always doing that.

"Do you want to know how to get them?" Sharon asked.

"Maybe," Andrew told her.

"It'll cost you fifty cents. I have a secret recipe for freckle juice," Sharon whispered.

"A secret recipe?"

"Uh huh."

Sharon's tongue reminded Andrew of a frog catching flies. He wondered if Sharon ever got a mouthful of bugs the way she opened her mouth and wiggled her tongue around. Andrew inspected Sharon's face. "You don't even have freckles!" he said.

"Look close," Sharon said. "I've got six on my nose."

"Big deal! A lot of good six'll do."

"You can get as many as you want. Six was enough for me. It all depends on how much freckle juice you drink."

Andrew didn't believe Sharon for a minute. Not one minute! There was no such thing as freckle juice. Andrew had never heard of it before!

2

That night Andrew had trouble sleeping. He kept thinking about freckle juice. Maybe the reason no one in his family had freckles was because no one knew the secret recipe. If they never even heard of freckle juice, then how could they have any freckles? It figured!

Andrew didn't like the idea of paying Sharon for anything. And fifty cents was a lot of money. It was five whole weeks of allowance! But he decided that if Sharon's recipe didn't work he'd ask for his money back. It was easy.

The next morning Andrew turned the combination of his safe-bank to just the right numbers. Four on

top and zero on the bottom. He took out five dimes. He wrapped them in a tissue and stuffed the whole thing in his pocket. He didn't have time to wash his ears or neck or anything. He wanted to see Sharon before the last bell rang.

"Bye Mom," Andrew called.

"Andrew Marcus! Wait a minute!" His mother hurried over to him. She almost tripped on her long bathrobe. The curlers in her hair scratched Andrew's face as she checked his ears and neck.

"Please Mom! Can't we skip it just this once?" Andrew begged.

Mrs. Marcus stepped away from Andrew. She pointed a finger at him. "Okay," she said. "I'll let you go this time. But tomorrow I'm looking again. And, Andrew, zip up your pants."

Andrew looked down. Zippers were a pain!

"This afternoon when you come home I'll be next door. Mrs. Burrows invited me over to play cards. You come get the key from me, okay?"

"Sure Mom. Okay."

Andrew raced to school. He could hardly wait to see the secret recipe. First he'd look at it, and if it didn't seem any good, he just wouldn't pay.

Sharon was already at her desk when Andrew arrived. He went right over to her.

"Did you bring it?" he asked.

"Bring what?" Sharon opened her eyes real wide.

"You know what! The secret recipe for freckle juice."

"Oh that! I have it—right here." Sharon patted her pocket.

"Well, let's see it."

"Do you have the fifty cents?" Sharon asked.

"Sure—right here." Andrew patted *his* pocket.

"I'm not going to show it to you until you pay," Sharon said.

Andrew shook his head. "Oh no! First I want to see it."

"Sorry, Andrew. A deal's a deal!" Sharon opened a book and pretended to read.

"Andrew Marcus!" Miss Kelly said. "Will you please sit down. The second bell just rang. This morning we'll begin with arithmetic. Nicky, please pass out the yellow paper. When you get your paper begin working on the problems on the board."

Andrew went to his seat. Then he took the tissue with the five dimes out of his pocket. He held it near the floor and aimed it toward Sharon.

She sat in the next row. Sharon stuck out her foot and stepped on the tissue. Then she slid it over until she could reach it with her hand.

She bent down and picked it up. Miss Kelly didn't notice.

Sharon counted the five dimes. Then she took a piece of folded-up white paper out of her pocket and threw it to Andrew.

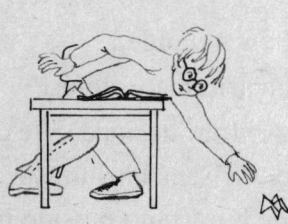

It landed in the middle of the aisle. Andrew leaned way over to pick it up. But he lost his balance and fell off his chair.

Everybody laughed, except Andrew and Miss Kelly.

Miss Kelly sighed. "Oh Andrew! What are you up to *now?* Bring me that note, please."

Andrew picked up the secret recipe. He didn't even have a chance to see it. It wasn't fair. It cost him fifty cents for nothing. He handed it to Miss Kelly. She read it. Then she looked up at him. "Andrew, you may have this back at three o'clock." She put it in her desk. "I don't want this to happen again. Do you understand?"

"Yes, Miss Kelly," Andrew mumbled.

"Good. Now let's get that arithmetic done."

Miss Kelly wasn't bad, Andrew decided. She could have ripped up the recipe. Or sent him to the principal's office. Or even made him stand outside in the hall by himself.

Andrew could hardly wait for three o'clock to come. He didn't bother counting Nicky Lane's freckles. Soon he'd have his own. When the second bell finally rang and the class marched down the hall, Andrew went up to Miss Kelly. She held the piece of white paper and waved it at him.

"Here's your note, Andrew. I have the feeling it's important to you. But from now on you must pay attention in class."

Andrew took the recipe from Miss Kelly. "After tomorrow I won't have any trouble paying attention," he promised. "Just you wait, Miss Kelly. I won't have any trouble at all!"

3

Andrew ran all the way home. Then he remembered he had to go to Mrs. Burrows' house to get the key. The secret recipe for freckle juice was folded carefully in the bottom of Andrew's shoe. He was going to put it inside his sock, but he was afraid if his foot got sweaty the ink might blur and he wouldn't be able to read it. So, inside his shoe was safe enough. Even if it was windy nothing could happen to it there. He made up his mind not to read it until he got home. He didn't want to waste any time getting there. And he wasn't the world's fastest reader anyway, even though he'd gotten better since last fall. Still, there

might be some hard words that would take a while to figure out.

Andrew pressed Mrs. Burrows' doorbell.

"Hello, Andrew," she said when she opened the door. "You're home from school early."

"I ran all the way," Andrew panted.

"How about some milk and cookies?" Mrs. Burrows asked.

"No thank you. I just want the key."

"Well, come in, Andrew. Your mother's in the living room."

Andrew followed Mrs. Burrows. His mother was dealing four piles of cards.

"Hi Mom. I came for the key."

"Manners, Andrew . . . manners! Don't you say hello to all the ladies?" Mrs. Marcus asked.

"Oh. Hello," Andrew said.

Mrs. Marcus reached for her purse. She opened it and gave Andrew the key. "Change your clothes and play outside. I'll be home by four o'clock."

That only gave him an hour. He hoped the recipe didn't say to cook anything. He wasn't allowed to turn on the stove or the oven. Andrew dashed to his house, unlocked the front door and took off his shoe as soon as he was inside. He pulled out the secret recipe and sat down on the floor to read it. It said:

Andrew read the list twice. It didn't sound like much of a secret recipe. His mother used those things every day. Of course, she didn't use them all *together*. Maybe that was the secret part. Well, he'd paid fifty cents. He might as well find out.

He climbed up on the kitchen counter so he could reach the cabinets. He found everything except the lemon—that was in the refrigerator—and the onion. Mrs. Marcus kept onions in the basement in a bin. Andrew ran downstairs and selected a small one, since the recipe only called for a speck. With or without the skin, Andrew wondered.

He chose a big blue glass. He'd start with just one glassful and then drink another if he wanted more freckles. No point in overdoing it the first time. That's what his mother always said.

Now, first the grape juice, Andrew thought. He filled the glass halfway and added an ice cube. All drinks tasted better cold and he was sure this one would too.

Then he added the other ingredients one by one. His mother had two kinds of vinegars—wine vinegar and plain vinegar. Andrew picked the wine one. He put in some hot mustard, one spoonful of mayonnaise and plenty of pepper and salt. Then some ketchup . . . that was hard to pour. But what about olive oil?

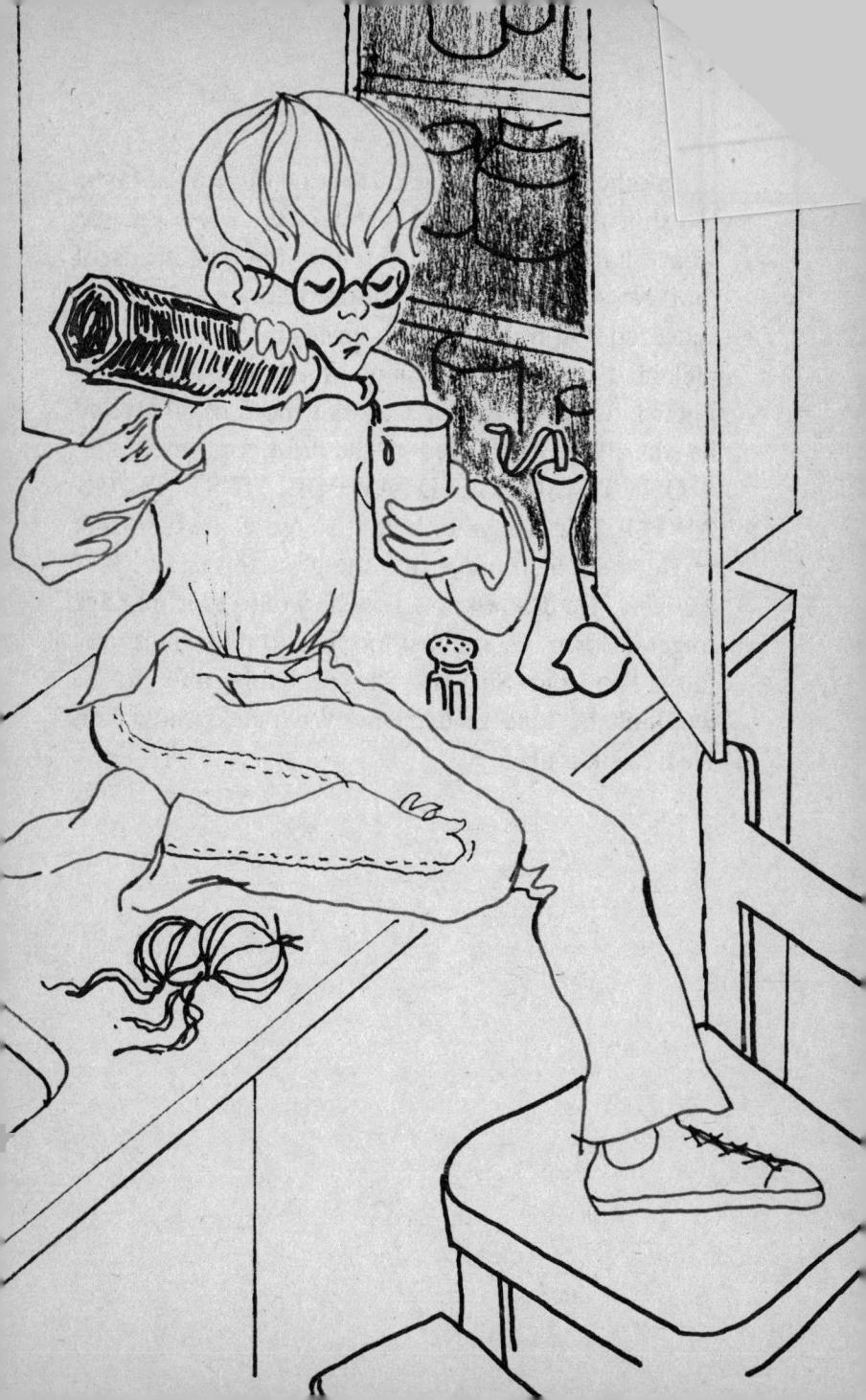

His mother had vegetable oil, but no olive oil. Maybe the stuff that looked like water in the olive jar was what Sharon meant. He put in a few spoonfuls of that. Now for the lemon. Andrew cut one in half and squeezed. Oh no! A seed dropped in by mistake. He picked it out with his spoon. He hated pits in his juice. Now all he needed was that speck of onion and he was all set. He stirred up the drink and smelled it.

OH! IT SMELLED AWFUL! JUST PLAIN AWFUL! He'd have to hold his nose while he drank it. He stuck his tongue into the glass to taste it. Ick! *Terrible!* He didn't know how he would ever manage to get it down . . . and fast too. It said to drink it very fast! That old Sharon! She probably thought he wouldn't be able to drink it. Well, he'd show her. He'd drink it all right!

Andrew held his nose, tilted his head back and gulped down Sharon's secret recipe for freckle juice. He felt like throwing up . . . it was that bad! But if he did he'd never get freckles. No, he would be strong!

Andrew crept into his mother's bedroom. He didn't feel well enough to walk. He sat on the floor in front of the full-length mirror. He waited for something to happen.

4

Pretty soon something happened, all right. Andrew turned greenish and felt very sick. His stomach hurt. At four o'clock Mrs. Marcus came home.

"Yoo hoo . . . Andrew. Where are you?" she called.

Andrew heard her but he couldn't answer. He was too weak. He made a small noise.

"Andrew Marcus! Is that you?" His mother stood in the doorway of her bedroom. "What are you doing in here? I told you to play outside! And why didn't you change your clothes? Didn't I say to change your clothes?"

Andrew made another noise. Mrs. Marcus looked

34

at his face. "Andrew, you're green. *Absolutely green!* Are you sick?"

Andrew nodded. He was afraid if he opened his mouth he'd lose the freckle juice.

"What hurts?" Mrs. Marcus asked, feeling his forehead.

Andrew moaned and held his stomach.

"Oh my! Appendicitis! *You must have appendicitis.* I'm going to call the doctor. No, I'd better just drive straight to the hospital. No, I'll call the ambulance!"

Andrew shook his head but his mother didn't notice.

She said, "Don't move. I'm going into the kitchen to phone. I'll be right back."

Andrew rolled around, moaning.

Mrs. Marcus came back to her bedroom in a hurry. "Andrew Marcus! I've just seen that mess in the kitchen. Did you or did you not make something and eat it?"

Oh-oh! He forgot to clean up. Now she knew. Well, he didn't care. His stomach was killing him.

"Well, young man! I'm surprised at you. *Surprised!* Mrs. Burrows offered you milk and cookies and you refused. Then you came home and made yourself an

... an I-don't-know-what and scared me half to death thinking you had appendicitis. I always thought you were more sensible, Andrew! I just can't believe it."

Andrew closed his eyes.

"Now, young man . . . *you* are going to *bed!*"

Andrew thought that was the best idea he'd heard in a long time. Mrs. Marcus gave him two spoonfuls of pink stuff that tasted like peppermint. Then she tucked him into bed.

Maybe the freckles would come out while he was sleeping. Right now he didn't care much if they *ever* came out! He hated Sharon. She'd done it on purpose. Just to get his fifty cents! He'd show her. She'd be sorry some day. He drifted off to sleep. He had terrible dreams. A big green monster made him drink two quarts of freckle juice, three times a day. Every time he drank it, the *monster* got freckles but Andrew didn't.

Andrew woke up sweaty. His stomach still felt funny. His mother gave him two more spoonfuls of that pink stuff and he fell asleep again.

The next day Andrew stayed home from school. He only looked in the mirror once—no freckles! He wasn't surprised. At noon he drank some hot tea. He wasn't ever going back to school. Sharon wasn't go-

ing to see him without freckles. She thought she was so great. Well, she wasn't going to get the chance to laugh at him. No sir!

But the following day his mother woke him up and sang, "Time for school. Rise and shine! Don't forget to wash your neck and behind your ears." She pulled the covers off him.

"I'm not going to school today," Andrew said. "I'm never going to school again." He hid his head under his pillow.

"So! I've got a school dropout in second grade. We'll have to do something about that! Here are your clothes. I want to see you up and dressed before I count to fifteen or you're going to take three baths a day *every* day for the next ten years!"

Andrew got dressed. He ate a breakfast bun and drank some milk. But he couldn't let Sharon get away with it. He had to do something!

5

After breakfast Andrew raced back to his bedroom. He opened his desk drawer and looked for a brown magic marker. All he could find was a blue one. It was getting late. Blue would have to do. He put the magic marker in his lunch box and headed for school. He stopped two blocks before he got there. He studied his reflection in a car window. Then he took out the magic marker and decorated his whole face and neck with blue dots. Maybe they didn't look like Nicky Lane's freckles, but they sure looked like something!

Andrew waited until the second bell rang. Then he hurried to his class and sat down. He took out a

book and tried to read it. He heard a lot of whispering but he didn't look up.

Miss Kelly snapped her fingers. "Let's settle down, children. Stop chattering." Everybody giggled. "What's so funny? Just what is so *funny?* Lisa, can you tell me the joke?"

Lisa stood up. "It's Andrew, Miss Kelly. Just look at Andrew Marcus!"

"Stand up, Andrew. Let me have a look at you," Miss Kelly said.

Andrew stood up.

"Good heavens, Andrew! What have you *done* to yourself?"

"I grew freckles, Miss Kelly. That's what!" Andrew knew his blue dots looked silly but he didn't care. He turned toward Sharon and stuck out his tongue. Sharon made a frog face at him.

Miss Kelly took a deep breath. "I see," she said. "You may sit down now, Andrew. Let's get on with our morning work."

At recess Nicky Lane turned around and said, "Whoever heard of blue freckles?"

Andrew didn't answer him. He sat in class all day with his blue freckles. A couple of times Miss Kelly looked at him kind of funny but she didn't say anything. Then at two o'clock she called him to her desk.

"Andrew," Miss Kelly said. "How would you like to use my secret formula for removing freckles?" Her voice was low, but not so low that the class couldn't hear.

"For free?" Andrew asked.

"Oh yes," Miss Kelly said. "For free."

Andrew scratched his head and thought it over.

Miss Kelly took a small package out of her desk.

She handed it to Andrew. "Now, don't open this until you get to the Boys' Room. Remember, it's a *secret formula*. Okay?"

"Okay," Andrew said.

He wanted to run to the Boys' Room, but he knew the rules. No running in the halls. So he walked as fast as he could. He couldn't wait to see what was in the package. Could there really be such a thing as freckle remover?

As soon as he was inside the Boys' Room he unwrapped the package. There was a note. Andrew read it. It said:

TURN ON WATER. WET MAGIC FRECKLE REMOVER AND RUB INTO FACE. RINSE. IF MAGIC FRECKLE REMOVER DOES NOT WORK FIRST TIME . . . TRY AGAIN. THREE TIMES SHOULD DO THE JOB.

MISS KELLY

Ha! Miss Kelly knew. She knew all the time. She knew his freckles weren't really freckles. But she didn't tell. Andrew followed Miss Kelly's directions. The magic freckle remover formula smelled like lemons. Andrew had to use it four times to get his freckles off. Then he wrapped it up and walked back to his classroom.

Miss Kelly smiled. "Well, Andrew. I see it worked."

"Yes, Miss Kelly. It sure did."

"You look fine now, Andrew. You know, I think you're a very handsome boy without freckles!"

"You *do?*"

"Yes, I do."

"Miss Kelly . . . Miss Kelly!" Nicky Lane called out, raising his hand and waving it all around.

"What is it, Nicky?" Miss Kelly asked.

"Could I use your magic freckle remover? Could I, Miss Kelly? I hate my freckles. I hate every single one of them!"

Andrew couldn't believe it. How could Nicky hate his freckles? They were so neat!

"Nicky," Miss Kelly said. "Andrew didn't look good with freckles. But you look wonderful! I'd hate to see you without them. They're part of you. So, I'm going to put away this magic formula. I hope I never have to use it again."

Well, Andrew thought. She'd never have to use it on *him*. He was *through* with freckles.

When the class lined up to go home Andrew heard Sharon whisper to Nicky. "I know how to get rid of them."

"Get rid of what?" Nicky asked.

"Your freckles."

"You do?"

"Sure. The secret recipe for removing freckles has been in my family for years. That's how come none of us have any. I'll sell it to you for fifty cents!"

Then Sharon walked up alongside Andrew. Before Andrew could say a word Sharon made a super-duper frog face just for him.